MW01141397

CHRISTMAS 2012

Love gamps

THE STAR GRAZERS

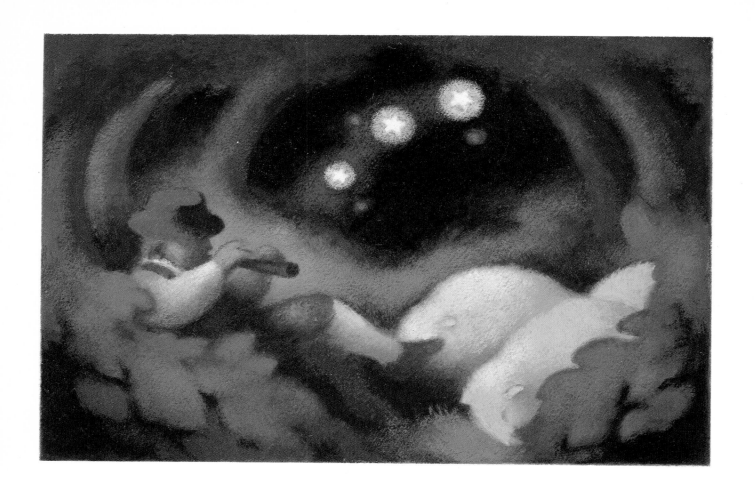

THE STAR GRAZERS

by CHRISTINE BARKER WIDMAN

illustrated by ROBIN SPOWART

Harper & Row, Publishers

The Star Grazers

Text copyright © 1989 by Christine Widman
Illustrations copyright © 1989 by Robin Spowart
Printed in the U.S.A. All rights reserved.
Typography by Carol Barr
10 9 8 7 6 5 4 3 2 1
First Edition

Library of Congress Cataloging-in-Publication Data
Widman, Christine.
  The star grazers / by Christine Widman : illustrated
by Robin Spowart. — 1st ed.
      p.   cm.
  Summary: Jacob the shepherd follows his sheep into
the sky, where Sirius the dog star protects them from
Lupus the wolf star while they graze on the stars in the
sky before returning home to sleep.
  ISBN 0-06-026472-1 : $
  ISBN 0-06-026473-X (lib. bdg.) : $
  [1. Stars—Fiction.   2. Sheep—Fiction.]
I. Spowart, Robin, ill.   II. Title.
PZ7.W6346St 1989   87-29377
[E]—dc19   CIP
                                              AC

To the brightest stars in my life—
Dennis, Matthew, Erin, Joshua, and Ashley
and, especially, to Doug
$$C.W.$$

To Marilyn

$$R.S.$$

Jacob is a shepherd boy. He is watching his sheep.

They run and leap...run and leap across a meadow
that stretches to the dark edge of the sky.

A gate appears. The sheep run and leap—one by one...
one by one—over the gate and into the sky.

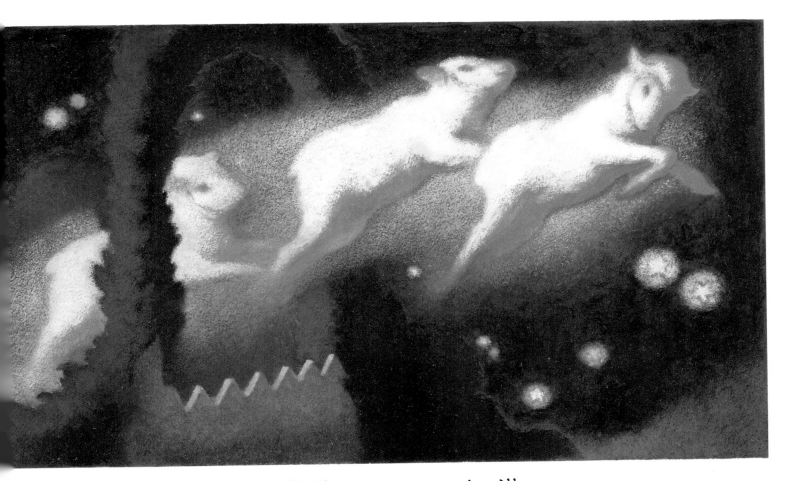

Jacob calls out, "Where are you going?"
The sheep baa back, "We are going to a meadow in the sky."

Jacob runs to the gate and opens it.
"I'm coming after you," he calls.
"You are my sheep, and I must tend you."
Up, up he follows the sheep.

In the sky meadow,
Jacob finds his sheep grazing on the stars.
"Why are you eating stars?" he asks.
"We are the star grazers," baa the sheep
as they nibble and munch,
nibble and crunch away the stars.
Their wool, filled with starlight,
begins to grow and grow.

"What is happening to you?" Jacob asks.
"Your wool is getting too long.
You must stop eating the stars."
"We cannot stop," baa the sheep.
"The stars are sweet—
sweeter than any meadow grass we have grazed on."

"But, my sheep, some stars are not sweet.
If you graze too far, Lupus, the Wolf Star,
will come out of the east and eat you."

A long howl rises from a faraway star.
"It is Lupus," Jacob whispers to the sheep.
"He smells you."

"Baa," the sheep bleat.
They begin to run, but their wool is so long,
it entangles their feet.
Jacob sees two eyes shining at the edge of the star field.
"Lupus!" he cries. "What shall I do?"
"Baa baa," cry the sheep.

"I can help," barks a white hound,
bounding out of the dark sky.
"I am Sirius, the Dog Star.
Lupus will not come near as long as
I am here to watch over you."
Jacob calls to his sheep, "Come quickly.
I need to crop your wool so you can walk home.
But what can I use to shear it?"

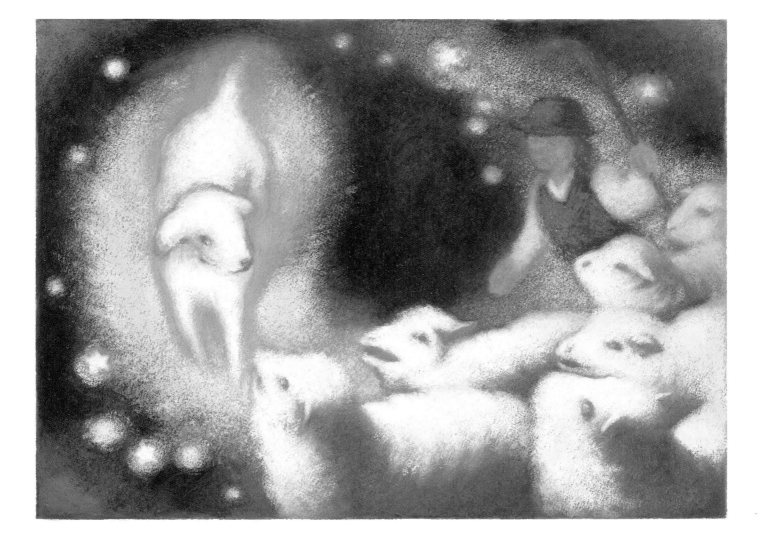

Jacob sees the knife-edged moon hanging in the sky.
He grabs the moon with one hand, and
holding a sheep with the other,
he pulls the sharp edge of the moon along the sheep's back.
The wool drops off, fluffy and white.
As Jacob fleeces each sheep,
the pile of wool grows higher and higher.
"I'm done," Jacob says. "It's time to go.
What can I carry your wool in?"
He turns the moon upside down.
"I will use this for my basket," he says,
putting the wool into the curve of the moon.

"Come, my sheep. I will lead you home."
Sirius barks and follows behind.

Down through the sky come Jacob and his sheep.
Fluffy white wool spills from the moon basket
and floats away.

At the edge of the sky, Jacob sees the gate.
He unlatches it, and one by one...
one by one...
his sheep leap and run across the meadow.
Jacob turns to say thank you to Sirius,
but the star dog is gone.
He looks in the moon basket.
The wool is gone, too.
"Good-bye," cries Jacob,
tossing the moon back to the sky.

He walks through the gate and across the meadow.
All his sheep lie fast asleep.

Jacob lies down too.
The grass is soft and sweet.
He watches the sky.
Clouds filled with starlight float across a crooked moon.
A white star hangs so low above the sleeping sheep
that Jacob sees silver in the short curls of their wool.
The bright star winks at Jacob.
Jacob smiles.
"Good night, Sirius," says the shepherd boy.